Once there was a girl
a very little girl.
And there was a dragon
a very biggle dragon.

They were friends…

EVERMORE DRAGON

Barbara Joosse

illustrated by Randy Cecil

WALKER BOOKS
AND SUBSIDIARIES

LONDON · BOSTON · SYDNEY · AUCKLAND

At the wake of derry-day
the friends decided what to play.
Hide-and-seek? Hide-and-seek!

OK, OK.

Dragon jumped up and down,
made a rum-below sound.

"Goodie, goodie, goodie!
Me first!"

Girl closed her eyes

so Dragon could hide.

Dragon found a little rock

   such a very little rock

and he curled his Dragon self

   his Drag-enormo self

into a dragon ball,

which wasn't – no, it wasn't – small at all!

Girl opened her eyes.

There was Dragon, yo ho.

But she climbed up a tree.

"Oh, where can Dragon be?"

And she peeked inside his lair.

"No, he isn't there."

And she stood upon a rock

such a very little rock

and she sighed a little sigh

such a very little sigh. Oh, my.

"Dragon's *so* good at hiding,

I'm not sure I can find him.

What to do?"

"BOO!"

Girl wrapped her arms around him

so everly around him.

"Oh, Dragon, you're so clever.

You're the smartest dragon ever."

And he knew

it was true.

"Now you!"

Girl ran

and ran

and ran …

to a faraway place

    such a hidey-hole place

and she didn't make a sound

    not a single little sound ...

shhhhh.

And she waited for Dragon

so long for Dragon

to be found by Dragon

and she stretched and she yawned and …

zzzzzzzz.

Dragon looked everywhere – every here, every there –

in the leaves

of the trees …

from the log

in the bog …

off the ridge of the bridge…

No Girl.

"Girl?" bellowed Dragon.
"Are you lost?" bellowed Dragon.

And she was.

Girl woke and it was night.

Deep, deep, dark night.

No stars. No moon.

No castle. No room.

No best friends together.

Just Girl.

Came the cricking and the cracking,

came the flipping and the flapping,

came the moaning and the groaning—

are there monsters in the night?

Oh, she tried so not to cry!

But she cried silver tears

    worry worry tears

and her heart thumped a sound

    a trem-below sound

that only Dragon friends,

very *very* special friends, can hear.

"Girl!" thundered Dragon.

"I hear you!" thundered Dragon.

And he breathed his dragon fire
and it lit up the sky
    made a bright night sky
and he flew through the night
All right!

"Girl!" roared Dragon.
    "I am here!" roared Dragon.

AND HE WAS!

Dragon wrapped his wings around her
so everly around her.
"I am here," rumbled Dragon.
"You're a dear," whispered Girl.

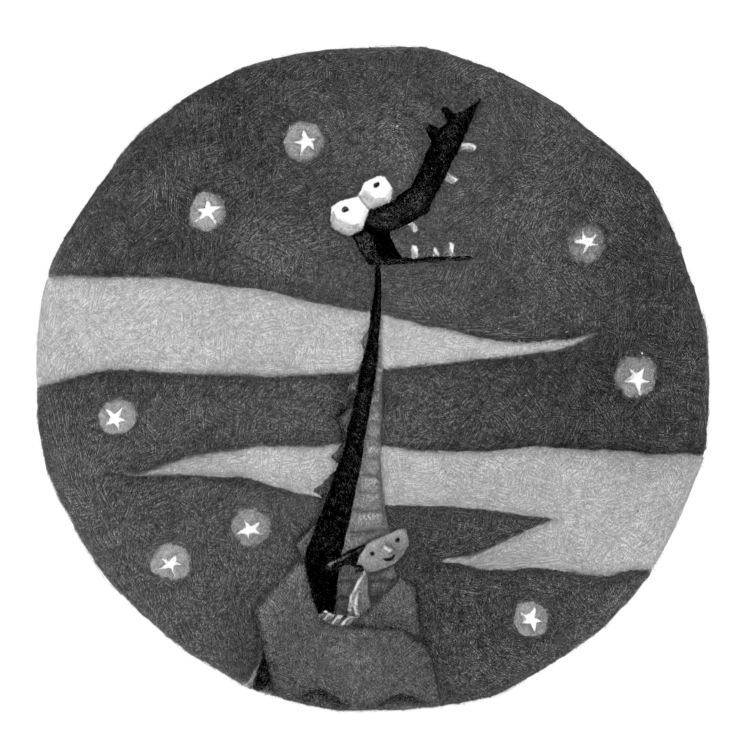

Dragon held her and he sang,

"Evermore, evermore, I am here."

And she knew

it was true.